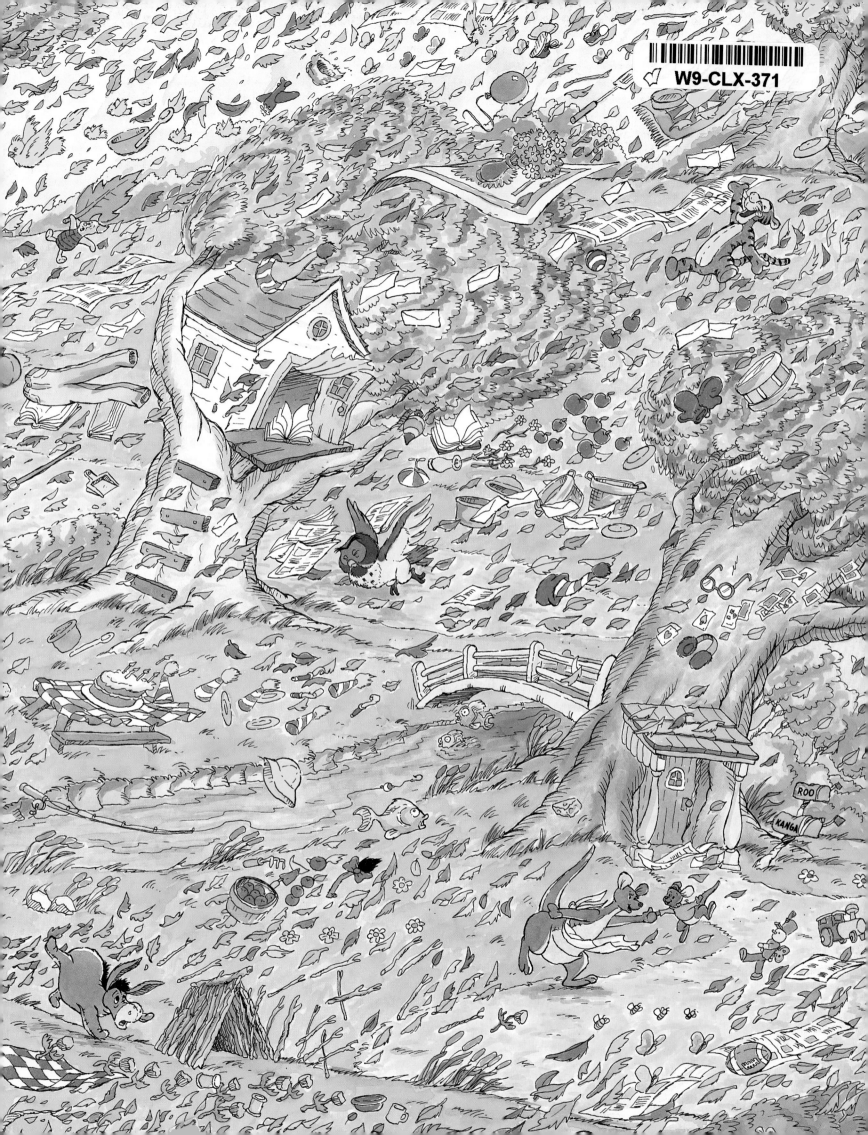

Poor Eeyore is sad because he thinks no one remembered his birthday. He doesn't know that Pooh and his friends are very busy. They are going to give Eeyore a birthday party he will never forget! Can you find these presents and party favors they have prepared?

A red balloon

A honey jar

A puppet

A paint set

A game

This party hat

This lollipop

This noisemaker

HIPY P

APAPY BTHUTHUDTH THUTHDA BTHUTHDY.

Silly old bear! Pooh ate every last drop of honey at Rabbit's house and he is so full he can't get out the door! As Pooh's friends try to free him, look and see if you can spot these things that are as round as Pooh's chubby tummy.

Orange

Vase

Teapot

Bubble

Tomato

Pillow

Doorknob

Silly old Pooh is frightened and has called all his friends to search the shadows for Heffalumps and Woozles. In the darkness, their sleepy eyes play tricks on them. Can you find these unscary items with very scary shadows?

Snail

Jacket

Rubber duck

Moth

Glove

Piggy bank

Toy soldier

Rope

MR SANDERZ

RNIG ALSO

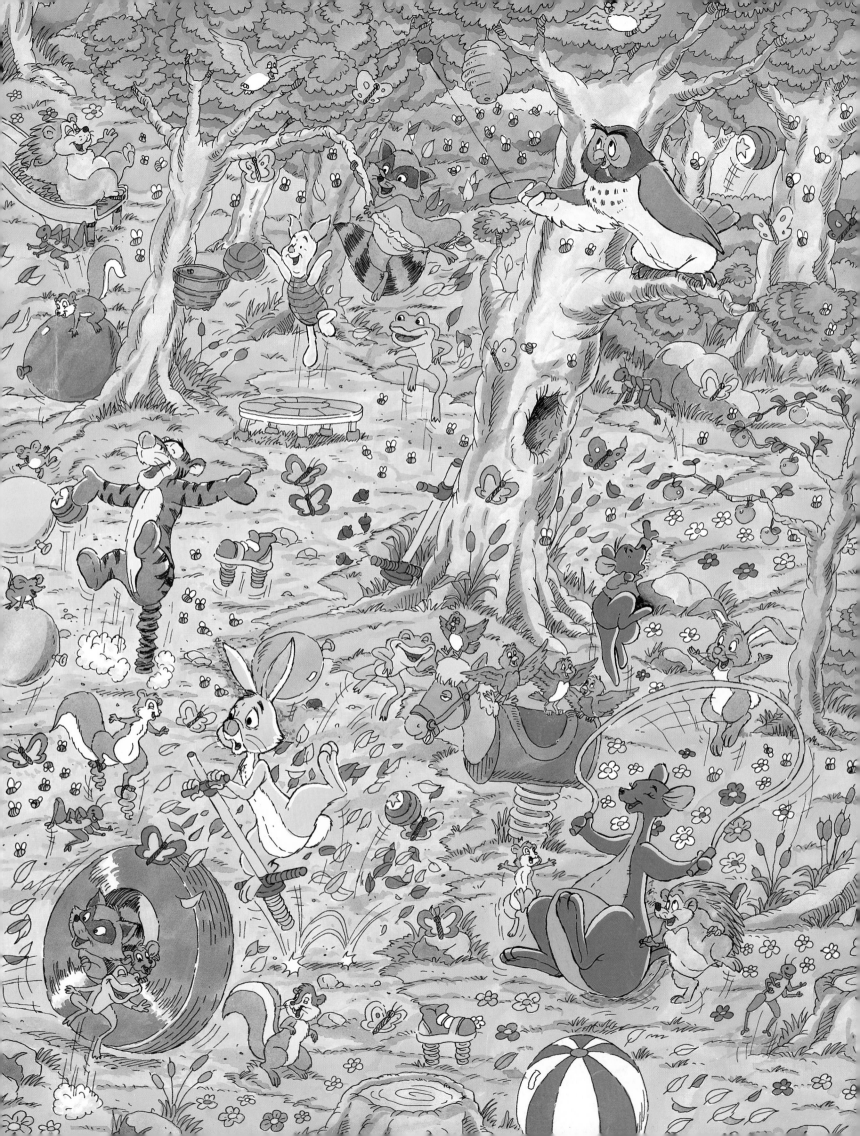

April fool! Today is April 1 and everything is topsy-turvy in the Hundred-Acre Wood today! Can you find these things that are in places where they do not belong? What else do you see that is not as it should be?

Bird

Cap

Pear

Ball of yarn

Beehive

Paintbrush

Toy boat

Hooray! The first snow fell last night! Pooh and his friends will spend the whole day having all sorts of winter fun. One of their favorite things to do is making snow sculptures. Can you find these lovable sculptures?

SnowPooh

SnowPiglet

SnowTigger

SnowRabbit

SnowEeyore

SnowKanga

SnowRoo

Pooh knows that where there are bees, there's honey! Boy, there are a lot of bees leading to the hive . . . and also a lot of Bs. Can you find these things that begin with the letter B?

Broom

Basket

Banana

Bluebird

Boomerang

Ball

Butterfly

Have you ever seen such fluffy clouds? Pooh and his friends love to look at them as they float by. Can you spot these cloud shapes that they have found? What other fun shapes can you see?

Bunny

Arrow

Honey jar

Duck

Teddy bear

Ice cream cone

Baby bootie

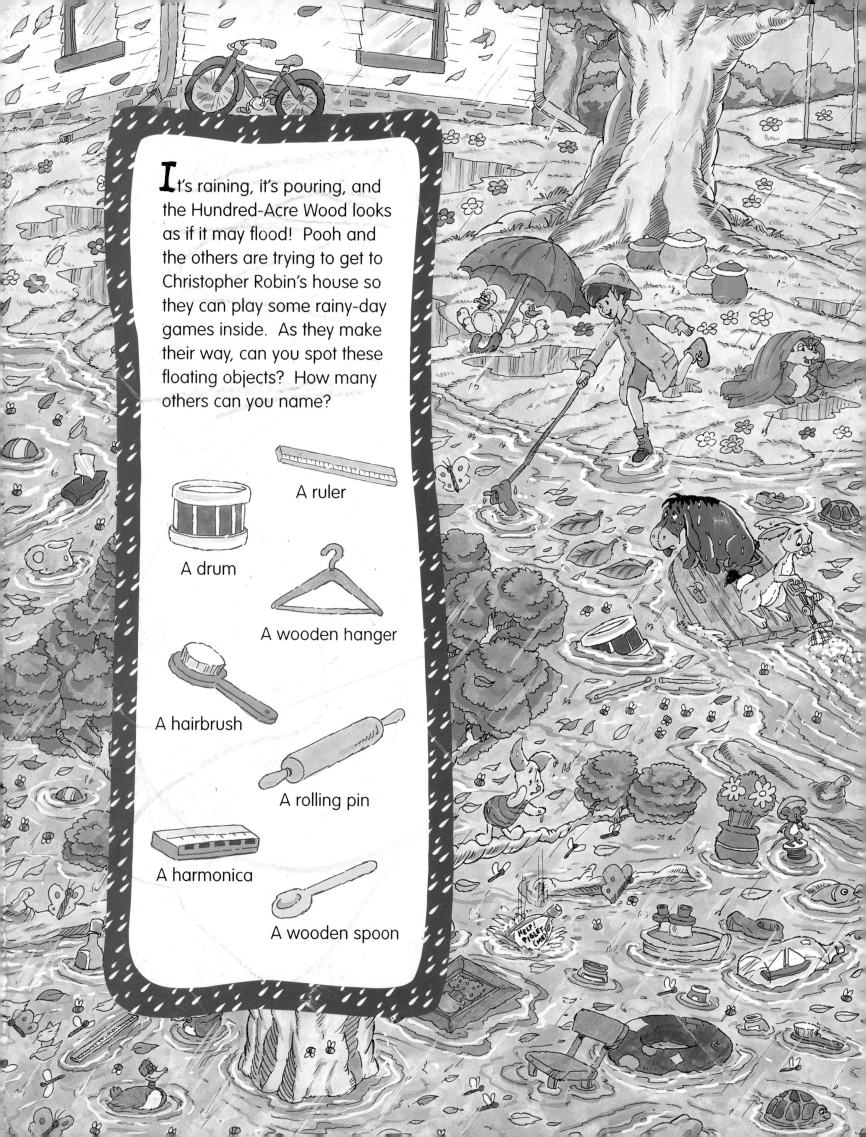

It's raining, it's pouring, and the Hundred-Acre Wood looks as if it may flood! Pooh and the others are trying to get to Christopher Robin's house so they can play some rainy-day games inside. As they make their way, can you spot these floating objects? How many others can you name?

A ruler

A drum

A wooden hanger

A hairbrush

A rolling pin

A harmonica

A wooden spoon

HELP! PIGLET (ME)!